TWENTY YAWNS

by Jane Smiley · illustrated by Lauren Castillo

SCHOLASTIC INC.

TO VERONICA—J.S.

FOR NOAH, ADAM, ALISON, AND MATT—L.C.

ISBN 978-1-338-17154-9

Text copyright © 2016 by Jane Smiley. Illustrations copyright © 2016 by Lauren Castillo.
Published in the United States by Amazon Publishing, 2016. This edition made possible
under a license arrangement originating with Amazon Publishing, www.apub.com.
All rights reserved. Published by Scholastic Inc., 557 Broadway, New York, NY 10012,
by arrangement with Amazon Publishing. SCHOLASTIC and associated logos are
trademarks and/or registered trademarks of Scholastic Inc.

12 11 10 9 8 7 6 5 4 3 2 1   17 18 19 20 21 22

Printed in the U.S.A.   08

This edition first printing, January 2017

Design by Sara Gillingham Studio
The artwork was created digitally with painted textures.

CAFE

The beach umbrella was flapping in the breeze.

flap!

Flap,

Not far from the waves, Lucy
was digging a hole all by herself.

Flap,

flap!

It got so big that her dad could lie down in it. When he did, she covered him up. They laughed and laughed.

Then he took her hand, and they ran
into the water. A big wave came in,
and he swung her into the sky.

Lucy walked with Mom and Dad

all the way to the end of the beach.

On the way back, Lucy rolled and
rolled down the soft warm dunes.

Even though she got dizzy and sandy,
she didn't want to stop.

Mom and Dad and Lucy stayed longer at the beach than they ever had before.

Lucy YAWNED.
Mom YAWNED.
Dad YAWNED.

Mom said, "Early bedtime!"

Outside Lucy's bedroom, the sun
was sinking below the horizon.
Strips of clouds were pink and red.

Lucy put her pajamas on inside out,
climbed into bed, and yawned a big

YAWN.

Mom began to read her a story. "Once upon a time, there lived a wonderful little boy named Fred. He was perfect in every way, or so his mother said." Lucy stretched and smiled.

She gave a big big big YAWN

and closed her eyes.

Mom stopped reading. She was asleep!

The moon shone through the window,
a silver veil that fell across the floor.
Everything looked mysterious, even
Lucy's own hands on the bedspread.
Suddenly, Lucy was wide awake.

She looked around. Everyone in
the pictures seemed to be watching
her—Grandma, Grandpa, Aunt
Elizabeth, Mom, and Dad.

Even Fred, in the book that
Mom had dropped on the floor.

Lucy slipped out of bed and padded to the door.
Her dad was snoring in the living room.

The house was **verrrrry** quiet.
Lucy needed Molasses, her bear.

He was wedged beneath
Hornet the giraffe,
Juno the horse,
Mathilda the alligator,
Frank the kangaroo,
and his baby, Leonard.

SWOOsh!

All the toys fell to the floor.

Lucy started to carry Molasses back to her bed. But the other toys were looking at her, even Leonard, the baby kangaroo. They seemed lonely.

So one by one,
she brought them
over to her bed
and dropped
them in a patch
of moonlight.

She spread her blankie over them and kissed them
good night. Now they looked sleepy and happy.

Lucy lay down and snuggled
in next to her friends,
sighed a big happy sigh, and

YAWNED.

She saw Fred,
the boy in the book,
YAWN.

She saw the moon
YAWN.

Lucy put her arms around Molasses. He seemed especially tired. Then she gave one last

YAWN. . . . and fell asleep.